NOT A BOX

Antoinette Portis

HarperCollins*Publishers*

Not a Box

Copyright © 2006 by Antoinette Portis

Printed in the United States of America.

All rights reserved. No part of this book may be used or reproduced in any manner whatsoever without
written permission except in the case of brief quotations embodied in critical articles and reviews. For information address
HarperCollins Children's Books, a division of HarperCollins Publishers, 1350 Avenue of the Americas, New York, NY 10019.
www.harpercollinschildrens.com

Library of Congress Cataloging-in-Publication Data is available.
ISBN-10: 0-06-112322-6 (trade bdg.) — ISBN-13: 978-0-06-112322-1 (trade bdg.)
ISBN-10: 0-06-112323-4 (lib. bdg.) — ISBN-13: 978-0-06-112323-8 (lib. bdg.)

Design by Antoinette Portis and Martha Rago
13 14 15 16 17 18 19 20
❖
First Edition

To children everywhere
sitting in cardboard boxes

Why are you sitting in a box?

It's not a box.

What are you doing on top of that box?

It's not a box!

Why are you squirting a box?

I said, it's not a box.

Now you're *wearing* a box?

This is not a box.

Are you still standing around in that box?

It's NOT NOT NOT NOT a box!

Well, what is it then?

It's my Not-a-Box!